What's So Scary?

by John Stadler

Orchard Books   New York

An Imprint of Scholastic Inc.

To all my friends at Orchard—J.S.

Orchard Books, an imprint of Scholastic Inc., 95 Madison Avenue, New York, NY 10016

Manufactured in the United States of America. Printed and bound by Phoenix Color Corp.

Book design by Mina Greenstein. The illustrations are brush, pen and ink, and watercolor. 10 9 8 7 6 5 4 3 2 1

Library of Congress Cataloging-in-Publication Data. Stadler, John. What's so scary? / by John Stadler. p. cm.
Summary: Animals drawn by an illustrator for a book try to figure out where they really belong.
ISBN 0-531-30301-2 (trade : alk. paper) [1. Animals—Fiction. 2. Books and reading—Fiction.
3. Artists—Fiction.] I. Title. PZ7.S77575 Wh 2001 [E]—dc21 99-87012

I'll tell you what's so scary. You drew me in the wrong book! I'm supposed to be in *Dog's Big Birthday Sleepover*. Look! You're dropping things all over the place. You look tired and overworked. Pull yourself together. Woe is me. I'm all alone with you on my birthday.

What's So Scary?
by John Stadler

Keep going!
Take it one page at a time.

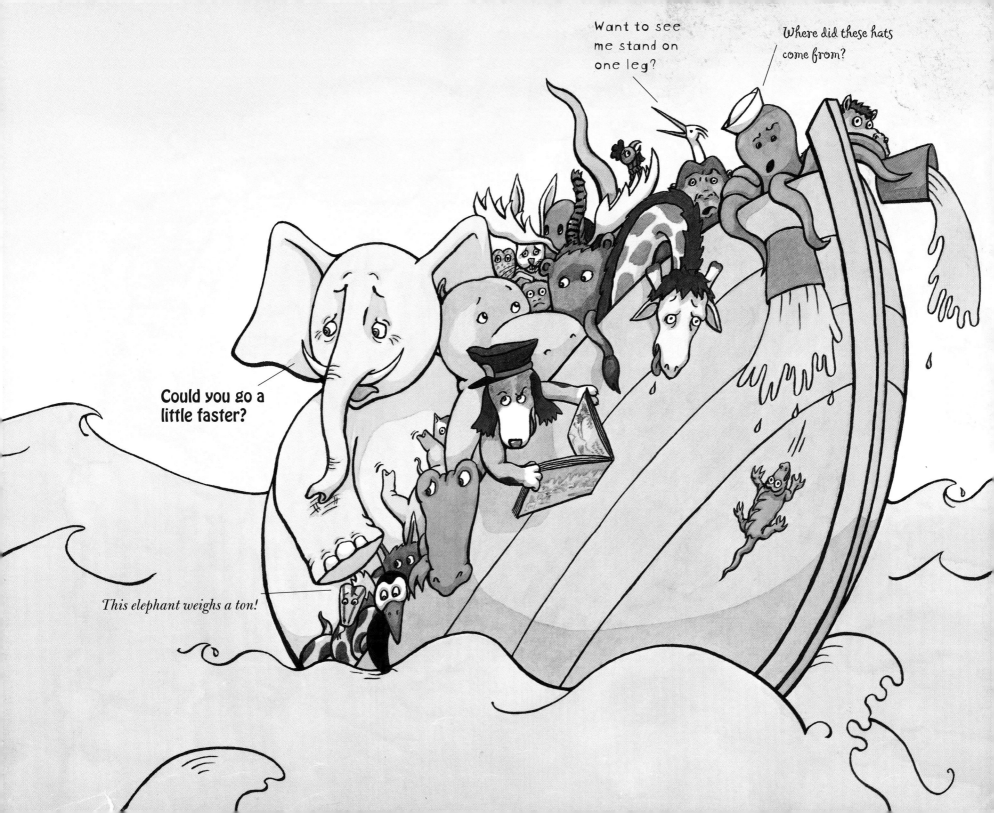

We can't go back.
A book goes only one way!
If we stay here any longer,
THE END will come now!

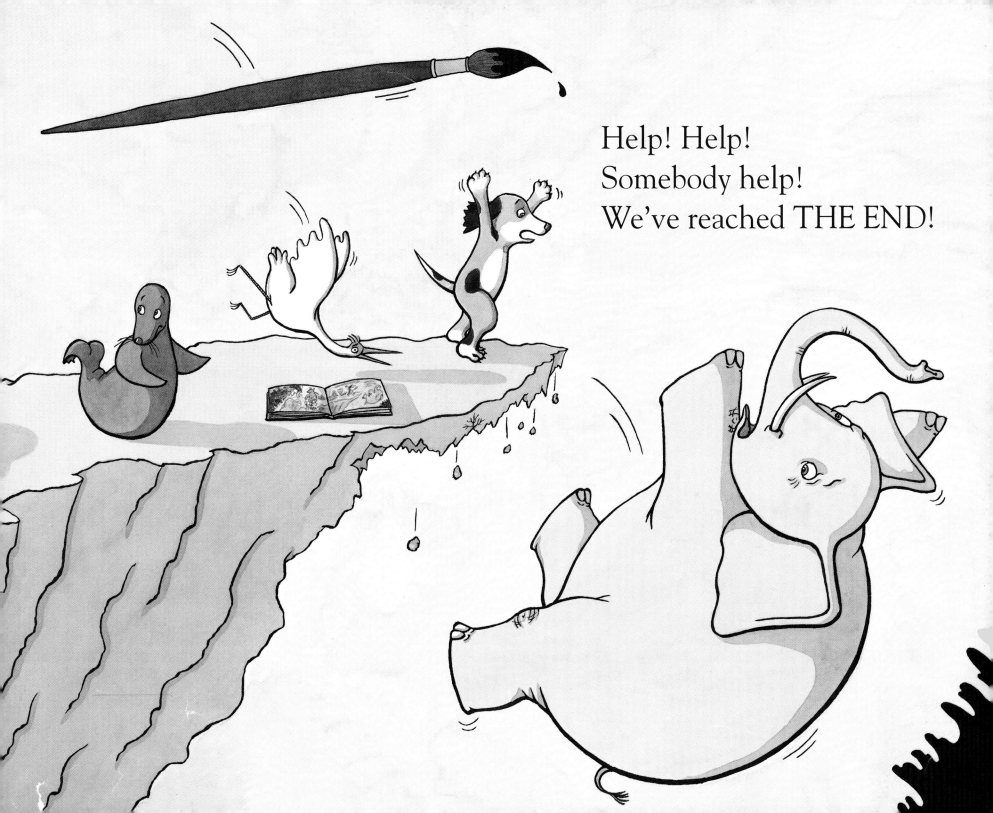

Help! Help!
Somebody help!
We've reached THE END!

What's this?
Hey, maybe it's time
to take things into my own hands.

What's so scary?

Scary? There's nothing to be scared of.
It's just the end of a story and the end of a day.
And I'm right where I always belonged,
in *Dog's Big Birthday Sleepover*.
So, all's well that ends well. GOOD NIGHT!

THE END

Wait! Since you're up,
can we have a glass of water?
And how about another story?